HEROES FALL

A Novella

by

Dylan Brody

Also by Dylan Brody

BOOKS

Laughs Last
The Warm Hello
A Tale of a Hero and the Song of her Sword
Xenophobia and the Jewish Druid

COMING SOON

Relatively Painless

CDs

True Enough
Brevity
A Twist of the Wit
Chronological Disorder
Write Large

All these and more available at
http://dylanbrody.com

First Printing, May 2009
Sam' s Dot Publishing

Second Printing January 2020
Active Voice Productions

This small book is for my wonderful wife Nancy who is, in fact, my one true hero. Without her there would be no book. There would be no chapters. There would be no paragraphs. Life would be a sentence. This book is for Nancy for whom I have fallen and for whom I fall again and again and who, by the grace of fate, seems to have fallen inexplicably for me.

HEROES FALL

I

His name was Kelsey Darson. He knew that. He repeated it to himself frequently. He introduced himself constantly. It was all that gave him a sense of sanity, a sense of self.

He looked down the hill at the burning house. A small group of neighbors had gathered. They watched as it burned. One of them did what she could to calm a woman who lived in the house. She screamed above the crackle of the flames. "My Baby!!" She screamed. "My boy's still in there!!" She struggled against the man who held her. She strained to return to the blazing building.

Kelsey did not stop to check his clothes, to find out what he was wearing or how it was fastened. He ran down the hill toward the fire. No weapon bounced at his hip.

He knew his job. It was all part of the Game. He was trying hard to learn the rules of the Game. He did not like the Game. He did not want any part of the Game. But somehow, he had become caught up in it, or it had caught him up. He was determined to handle the madness of it all. He would learn the rules of the Game. All of them. He would win and be done with it. If there was a way to win he would find it. He would find it in the rules.

Skirting the edge of the gathered crowd, Kelsey moved fast. He overleaped the front steps and, finding the front door locked, threw himself in through the window. The glass was a little thicker than he expected and the impact greater, but he was through and inside, the flames dancing about him, the ceiling above him fully engulfed. His eyes watered and the air was hot and thick with smoke.

He had tried, some time back, not playing the game. As he found himself in new surroundings, he ignored the obvious and pressing need of the moment. He offered no help to anyone and stood as an observer in the crises he encountered. People died. People he could have saved. A war began in one place, which he had not even known was the threat at hand. Still, each crisis was left behind when he was thrown to some new place to fulfill some new need. When he knew inaction would not put a stop to the horror of his situation, he again took up the habit of action and assistance. Better he should risk his life than risk a life plagued with guilt.

Hearing the coughing cry of a young child he moved through a fiery doorway toward the back. The heat intensified and the smoke became so deadly that he was forced to crawl beneath the airless cloud. He found the child trapped and frightened. Dragging him at first, then carrying him out, Kelsey performed a rescue that would be remembered in that town for centuries to come.

The house collapsed upon itself behind him. Spitting soot, his hands and face black with smoke and carbon, he handed the child to its sobbing mother. She thanked him, but never really looked at his face. Her focus was on her son, alive and pressed against her in a hug.

"I'm Kelsey Darson," he told her. Wiping his face with his sleeve he found his shirt was of very soft cotton. The seams were uneven, hand sewn.

She thanked him again without looking, her last words muffled by the child's hair.

The townsfolk moved toward him to thank him and meet him. The sensation began again, and he saw the faces go puzzled. He wondered again what the phenomenon looked like. The Fall began.

****

The Fall and the sensations in it had to be pieces of the puzzle that was the Game. As frightening as it had been at first, the feeling of the Fall became a point of fascination for Kelsey, a thing well worthy of examination and study.

It began with a slightly drunken sensation of removal and distance from the world around him. A heightened awareness of his alien-ness in his surroundings, his aloneness in his travels, would bring him to the brink of melancholy. Then, sharply, the world was pulled away from him. His vision shifted as through the wrong end of the binoculars. If there were sounds as the Fall began they dopplered as new sounds sharpened to replace them.

There was an extended moment at the heart of the Fall. Perhaps it was a split second of suspended time, perhaps an eternity collapsed into a milk carton.

A vague, tingling heaviness filled his body then, and though he tried on occasion to look down at himself during this transition, he could not. His focus, dreamlike, was decided for him and he could not tear it from the distant point of light that was the world toward which he plummeted. That point of light never grew but somehow approached at once and, with a snap which he learned was not painful if he did not struggle, became that waking dream, reality.

****

Facing a new reality each time, every few minutes or hours, Kelsey found that new clothes, new people, a new challenge had all become routine. Just as the walk from his dingy apartment to the bookstore on forty-third street had been routine once, falling from one world to another had now become a matter of course, the daily grind, the start of a new job.

The sky here was green. His clothes were almost Elizabethan, but the technology more developed. His tights were of a soft, manufactured fabric, and where a sword would hang he carried an odd, plastic device with a button on top and a small knob. It reminded him of his old electric razor.

He felt accumulated beard growth at his neck and cheeks. The last time he had shaved he had been in an odd Inn under a double-mooned sky. He decided he would shave at the next opportune moment.

As there was no apparent immediate threat, this was the first available moment. He set out in search of a hotel.

He felt at himself as he walked, searching for pockets. Instead he found a leather sack hanging opposite his weapon, at his right hip. He opened it and found his journal still with him, still intact. He determined then to find out if he could carry a razor with him as well. He opened his journal and read a few lines to himself just to see what the language of this place looked like and to hear how it sounded from his lips.

He was in a small city. The buildings were tall and seemed taller still, for they were very narrow.

A woman approached him directly. This was new. Before she spoke, Kelsey guessed that she was connected to his job in this place.

Her hair was dark and flecked with gray. Her eyes were sharp blue and very serious. Deep shadows underlined them and the creases pointing toward their corners did not suggest laughter so much as a continuous flinch.

"Kelsey!" she said, and took his hand. "I got here as fast as I could. I had to get a lost kid off a roof a few blocks away." With that she pulled a flat, rectangular stone from a vest pocket and handed it to him. "Here's your razor. You rub the flat side against the hair."

Confused, he experimented and it worked. He spoke as he took off the beard. "You know me. You know my thoughts."

"What? Uh. Kind of. What is it, Kelse?"

"Who are you? How do you know me? What are the rules?"

Her eyes widened and she took him by the arm, firmly. She examined his face as the fur fell away. "You're so young, Kelsey. You've never met me before, have you?"

He examined her face as closely, shaking his head. He slipped the shaving stone inside the wide seam of his vest. It fit well there.

"Wow. Okay, kiddo. My name's Salia. Do you know what you're here to do yet?"

"No." He told her. "Wait. Are you falling, too?"

"All the damn time. Come on. Let's get out of the city. Maybe we can forestall the Fall, somehow. Get some time to talk."

Out of the city sounded good to him. He nodded and allowed her to pull him back along the road the way he'd come.

"Do you know what's happening to me?"

And now she laughed. She laughed easily, though it made her eyes look a little as though she was flinching. "No. Yes. Right now I know about as much as you'll ever know. I am a heroine. You are a hero. We fall from place to place and do what heroes and heroines do. You and I fall to a lot of the same places and meet up a lot of the time. Are you with me so far?"

"No. Sorry. If we meet up a lot, how come I've never met you?"

"'cause we don't reach these worlds and places and times in the same order. Look. Let's say I--"

She started at the sound of an enormous explosion. The bright light against her face shadowed deeply near her eyes.

Kelsey spun around in time to see the fragile building fall. The screams began before the dust had cleared and Kelsey ran to do his job. He turned once to shout last words to Salia, but she was already gone... falling somewhere probably.

He choked through the powdery air, digging with his hands and cutting with the weapon that he carried to become part of a mass rescue.

When all the survivors were free of the rubble and all of the injured under care, Kelsey sat upon a flight of narrow steps a block away and let his eyes drift closed.

****

<u>II</u>

Sleep only came when exhaustion was complete. It was always filled with dreams of falling. It always left him in a new surrounding. From the first time this occurred Kelsey wondered how he could have slept through a Fall, how tired must his mind have been to shut out even such a feeling from his perception.

Once he had awakened briefly from a deep sleep. He thought that he saw someone sitting nearby, a woman with a musket at her shoulder. It had returned to him in memory some time later and he thought it to have been a dream.

Now when he awoke a new thought came to him. He thought that in his sleep, perhaps, he fell through many worlds. He feared that his own selfish need for sleep might leave him slumbering through crises; people might be dying, screaming all around as he, a grown up infant, unaware, slept through from world to world.

He opened up his journal and put the thoughts on paper.

"Ho there, Bastard." A voice came to him. He put the journal away and stood up.

The voice came from a tall, thin man with a dark beard and one eyebrow that became just a little less dense as it crossed the bridge of his nose. The man held a sword threateningly.

Kelsey found one at his own hip and drew it sharply. "What can I do for you?"

"Tell me what you meant about the Oak Tree."

"What?"

"Tell me or die. I've had your woman. You've admitted that some day I'll slay you. Now tell me what you meant by that one cryptic little remark and I'll spare your life."

"What woman? I don't have a woman. Leave me alone!"

The man approached steadily, so Kelsey slapped away the blade with his own. This seemed only to anger the man and he made a sharp thrust that Kelsey could not parry in time. It caught him in the thigh and a dull throbbing pain followed as his assailant withdrew the weapon.

"What the hell is the matter with you?" Kelsey shouted over the pounding that had suddenly filled his ears. "Who are you? What do you want?"

The man raised his eyebrows. "Name's Mordak, Kelsey. And you--"

But the world was already receding far too fast for Kelsey to understand his words.

****

A gravelly road was built up between two, slightly lower gravelly plains. Scattered pools of water decorated the barren landscape. Far away down the road a lone figure walked. The distance was too great to tell whether the figure approached or receded.

Taking a moment to tear a bandaging strip from his shirt (wooly now, but soft) Kelsey walked toward the figure, limping on his wrapped and injured leg. He wondered what danger, what crisis might present itself here.

"Kelsey?" The figure called to him and he recognized the voice as Salia's.

At the horizon's lip a formation of five small, jet-like planes cut the sky in a Vee formation, coming up behind Salia with a deep roar. They looked a bit like pterodactyls.

He began to jog toward her, his leg throbbing with the effort; but even as he sped up, she began to recede and the world around him with her.

This was a first. No crisis. No danger. Just a short stop over, then the Fall.

****

A blue sky with white clouds gave Kelsey a feeling of 'home.' Horses that looked like horses trotted by.

The roll and rumble of the ocean sounded just like the roll and rumble of the ocean. The air smelled of flowers and trees.

On a cliff overlooking the water a castle was built of corral and sandstone. As it was the only building in sight, Kelsey climbed toward it.

Five gull-like birds cut the sky in formation. Kelsey noted the connection to his last stop. This had to be a clue, a piece of the puzzle.

He came to the castle's entryway and looked for a way to knock. A small panel in the door opened and a man looked out at him.

"Can I help you?" The man asked in the language of the land.

"Maybe. My name's Kelsey Darson. I think I'm supposed to be here."

"Kelsey?!?" Her voice came from above this time and Kelsey looked up to see Salia leaning over the edge of the highest parapet. "Salia?" He shouted up to her.

"Let him in!" She yelled. "He's with me!"

The small panel closed. The big door opened. A guard took away the small knife which hung at Kelsey's hip and he was escorted inside to a sort of waiting room.

Salia joined him shortly.

"Thank God," He said. "Now. What were you saying?"

"When?"

He noticed that her eyes were less creased, her hair just beginning to show gray. "When I talked to you last."

She laughed. "This is still pretty new to you, Huh?"

"What?"

"Look. There's an attack coming from the sea. The ships have already been spotted on the horizon and every one here is afraid to man the catapults on the roof."

"Why?"

"Superstition about the gulls. I've been here for a few days. I was hoping you'd show up. This is gonna be one hell of a fight."

She started off through a doorway and down a long hall. Kelsey followed her. "What were you telling me about not finding these places in the same order?"

"When, Kelsey? Look. I don't know where you're coming in from. You look real young. You're going to have to be more specific."

"We were in a city with really tall buildings."

"I don't think I've been there yet, Kelse. This way."

She turned down a wider corridor and headed for the spiral stairs at its far end.

"What are you talking about? I just saw you there."

She took the steps two at a time, and Kelsey asked her to slow down. His leg was still bleeding a little and the muscle felt stiff and tired.

"But I looked older. Right?"

"Yeah."

"I was older. Look. The last time I saw you, you had gray hair and you bawled like a baby by the pond. You remember it?"

"What? When?"

"See? You haven't done it yet. You're young."

A door at the top of the stairs led them onto the roof. Three catapults were loaded and pulled. Salia showed him how to release the catches and they waited, side by side, with the sun at their backs, manning the catapults.

After a long silence he said, "So you know my future?"

"Pieces of it. Just like you know I'm going to meet you some day in a place with tall buildings. Is there anything I have to remember when I get there?"

"I don't know. You could try to remember to bring me a razor."

"What for?"

"So I can shave."

"Oh." She pointed out to sea. "There they are. They'll be within range when they reach the far end of the tower's shadow."

"Do we ever get to finish a conversation?"

"We had a chance once that I can remember. But we didn't wind up finishing."

"Why not?"

"We made love instead."

He looked at her differently, now. She was attractive. Her hair caught the wind.

She released the catch and a big boulder sailed above the ocean toward the approaching tall ships.

There was a distant sound of cannon fire and the world erupted into war.

They had no time to chat again. The battle burned and burst all night. When at last a moment of quiet came and only one boat remained, Salia fell away and Kelsey was falling.

****

Under a sky of brooding grey Kelsey walked along the beach. He spotted Salia's lithe form on the rocks above him. He shouted to her and she turned at his voice.

His voice sounded high and tinny in the thin air. The language he spoke was whistling and airy. She came down the rocks to him. The creases at her eyes were back, but not so deep as they'd been that first time. Her hair had not yet begun to lose its luster.

"How you holding up, Kiddo? Where are you coming in from?"

"We just defended a castle. Overlooking an ocean."

Her eyes grew a little misty as she looked out over the ocean. "I remember it. That was a long time ago."

"Lucky you. My ears are still ringing."

"Lucky you. Two oceans in a row. I've been in deserts for three Falls running."

"Yeah. Two oceans in a row. I think I'm beginning to put together a pattern."

Salia laughed richly, like a parent laughing when a child says he'll grow up to be a super hero.

"What's funny?"

"One of the first things you ever told me was that there is no pattern. Or if there is it's indiscernible."

"I was wrong."

"You were old. You were on your way to-- you were old."

They both fell silent for a moment, walking. Coming around a rocky outcropping they discovered a big sand-sculpture of a sea animal. It had the look of a lion with the flippers of a seal. It did not look at all like a Sea Lion.

"Oh boy. Get down." Salia lay on her stomach and Kelsey imitated.

"Why are we lying down?"

"I don't know. You warned me about this."

Flame spouted from the lion's mouth. It passed harmlessly above their backs.

"You see?" She added. "Split off and flank."

They did.

Coming in from the seaward side of the lion statue, Kelsey stayed low and felt at his hip for a weapon. There was none there. He remembered the knife that was taken from him at the castle.

Mordak emerged from the beast's back like a gunner coming through the turret of a tank. He aimed a weapon at Kelsey. At once the hero dove, rolling on the sand as flame, much less than that from the lion's mouth but just as hot, seared across the bright sand. It took him a moment to reclaim his footing on the soft surface.

When he did he saw that Salia had already climbed up from the far side. Her right arm locked around Mordak's throat and the man dropped his weapon. It bounced once on the haunches of the sand creature before coming to rest below him.

There was fire in Salia's eyes. Fire and fury. The kind that only come when long awaited revenge is in sight. She tightened her headlock, twisting.

Kelsey was sure his troubles with Mordak were about to be over. Any moment now his neck would snap.

The snap did not come. Salia shrank away suddenly as if running backwards into the distance. Then she was gone.

Mordak grinned at Kelsey. He was missing a tooth and his temples were shocked with white.

Kelsey took the last couple of steps toward him and scooped the weapon up from the beach. He aimed it at Mordak.

"I've got some questions to ask you," He said.

But Mordak fell back, vanishing as if with great distance.

Angry, frustrated, Kelsey kicked at the sand sculpture until the head fell off revealing the long barrel of a disgui sed flame weapon. Cheers came from the cliffs to the east.

A group of people, all very excited, ran toward him.

"He's slain it!" One of them shouted. "He's slain the sand dragon!!!"

Kelsey let out a long slow breath and turned to face the sea. The sea and the beach began to recede.

****

III

A wide-winged reptile banked lazily against orange clouds. Kelsey held a heavy broadsword. He found a frog for it at his belt and put the sword away.

The forest was lush and quiet. He heard no screams, sensed no danger. He chose a direction and began to walk.

Something stirred in the brush to his right. He turned in time to see Salia growing swiftly as if from some great distance. She lay on her side and for a moment he thought she might be injured or dead. When she had reached her natural proportions he saw that she was asleep.

He moved to wake her, to ask questions and talk. He thought better. He sat beside her, drawing his sword and laying it across his knees. He guarded her that way for hours as she slept. He used much of the time to write in his journal of the patterns he'd begun to piece together.

A wolf-like creature approached at sunset. It sniffed and growled about the fire Kelsey had built. When Kelsey ran at it with his gleaming blade it took off into the night.

He fell away then, hoping Salia would sleep safely without him.

****

Kelsey fell through a number of places in a row in which Salia slept. He saw her at many different ages, sleeping. He sat guard diligently for her, and when defense was needed he gave it. He grew very tired, but he continued his duty until he thought he no longer could.

Then he fell to a place where he was quite busy.

****

The gun was of flint-lock design with two barrels.

The Pattern of Travel Theory had fallen apart when nothing wolf-like showed up.

The ship beneath him lifted and rolled with the ocean's swells.

"Ho, there," a seaman called out. "Where did you come from?"

"I'm not sure," Kelsey shouted. "My name is Kelsey Darson."

Before the man had time to ask more questions, a call from the crow's nest told him there was a ship to the port. As Kelsey saw no ship, he figured port must mean 'left'. He ran to the opposite side of the ship. His figuring proved correct.

Cannon fire boomed around him as a smaller pirate vessel pulled along side the ship. The poorly clad crew of rogues heaved grappling hooks, latching their ship to the one that bore Kelsey.

He drew steel. His blade was light now and curved.

"What's the job, Darson?" Salia asked.

She was just behind him and to his right. When he turned he saw that she held a similar blade. She was very young and her eyes were bright and sharp.

"Looks like a pirate boarding."

"Got it. Let's fight some bad guys."

"Good attitude," Kelsey said. "Let's fight some bad guys."

Kelsey fought bad guys for over an hour. For the first time since the Game began, Kelsey enjoyed himself thoroughly. There was a beautiful young woman at his side. His steel flashed and rang in confrontation. The sun set gold on the ocean and silver on his blade. The sea swelled red with blood and sharks circled the battle.

When he could see Salia she fought well and happily, a grin plastered across her face. He realized at one point that a similar grin was plastered across his own.

For a moment he thought he might actually be winning the Game. A moment was all he had to think this, for there were thrusts to be parried.

One of the crew set about cutting the pirates' lines. The cannon blasted into the attacking ship. In time the ships parted and the last of the pirates were dispatched.

The sky hung clear and moonless, but the stars were bright and many and they reflected against the sea.

Salia did not vanish. Kelsey did not vanish. They stood together on the deck. Crewmen celebrated around them. One of them handed Kelsey some dried beef. He ate it hungrily and drank their ale, but he did not socialize. He stood with Salia.

"You look young, Salia."

"I am young, Kelsey. You want to finish what you were telling me back there?"

"When?"

"About keeping a journal."

"I told you about my journal?"

"You started to. Then you disappeared. You said eventually it was going to make sense of what's been happening to us."

"I did?"

"You did."

"But *you* said that I said that there was no discernible pattern."

"I did?"

"You did."

Salia pondered this for a moment. Kelsey pretended to ponder, but spent the time examining the lift of Salia'a hair in the starlight.

That damned voice cut in on them. "Damn, Kelsey! What does it take to kill you?"

"Who's that?" Salia asked.

"That's Mordak. He doesn't like us very much."

"Why?"

"I don't know yet."

Again Kelsey drew his steel.

"Damn," Salia said. "Good luck. I think I'm--" and she fell away.

Mordak set to him with a flashing vengeance. He cut hard and angrily at Kelsey forcing him back toward the ship's rail.

A few of the reveling crew members gathered to watch the fight.

Kelsey was very tired. He knew he needed sleep. If only he could keep parrying until he fell. He hadn't the strength left to mount a decent assault.

He leaned against the rail to steady himself, but it had been damaged in the battle with the pirates. It cracked beneath his weight and he fell back toward the water. He pulled a deep breath.

As he fell, he fell.

It was most unnerving, and quite a relief at the same time.

Man, he thought. *I hate this game.*

****

IV

Panic struck Kelsey when he fell into water. He knew it was not the shark infested water toward which he had been falling a moment earlier, but he was afraid, for an irrational instant, that this was a world of water without end, that perhaps there was no surface.

Holding his breath he focused on a distant light and swam toward it. It was a sun and there was plenty of air between it and the water.

Kelsey sucked that air in -- at first for life, then for the sheer pleasure of it. The water was warm. The sun was bright and familiarly yellow. The breeze was filled with pine and birch. He floated on his back. He breathed. He basked.

At last he pointed himself toward a grassy shoreline and kicked gently with his feet. He came up onto the grass and lay back. He did not yet let himself sleep. He absorbed his surroundings for a time first. The sweet wind. The soft turf. He wanted to stay awake longer, to enjoy the pleasure of this world.

He lost this battle. His eyelids dropped and he knew he would risk sleeping through his time in this beautiful place.

Sweet dreams came to him. He fought pirates on fifth avenue with swords and then went home to his apartment where he lived with Salia. In the dream it all seemed very natural and homey. There was a beautiful pond in his kitchen and they sat beside the pond while he cooked fish at the stove. Mordak came to the door to give him a religious magazine but he did not open the door and Mordak went away. Knowing his enemy would not return, he led Salia to the bedroom where there was a pond and a fish dinner. They made love in the pond, then they ate the dinner.

When he awoke he had not fallen. He had slept for hours and had not fallen. The pond was still there. The breezes still wafted coolly. Salia was there, too. She had built a fire and had caught a few fish and laid them out on the hot rocks around the blaze. Kelsey sat up.

"Good morning," he said.

"Good morning," she said. "Good to talk to you again."

"What's that mean?"

"I keep finding you when you're asleep. I've been sitting guard forever it seems."

"I've been there," he replied.

"I know."

"Have you figured out the job here, yet?"

She looked at him, then. Studied him. "There is no job here, Kelsey. There never is."

"You've been here before?"

"Yes. And you will have been, too. As far as I can tell it's the only stop we repeat."

Kelsey laughed. There was nothing else he could do. On the one hand the repetition of this one place completely shot to hell his latest developing theory.

On the other hand, the repetition of this one glorious place gave him something to hold on to. Some sense of time . . . of future . . . of hope.

The breeze moved Salia's hair in that way again and the touches of gray didn't make any difference. "Come here," he said.

"Are you sure?" Salia asked. "You look awfully young. You probably have a lot of questions." And she moved to him to let him take her in his arms.

"Questions can wait."

He kissed her neck softly, lowering her to the lush lawn. They made love in the grass. They made love sweetly. They made love happily. They made love in the pond.

They ate the fish.

Kelsey experienced a deja vu he could not explain. Then he fell.

****

V

It might have been bright night or dim day. Kelsey did not know. The sky was a constant blaze of streaking, swirling colors.

Endless sand stretched in all directions fading into reflective mirage toward the horizons.

Kelsey held a rock in his right hand. He turned slowly, seeking a break in the flat plain.

For an instant he thought someone approached from far away, but the approach was far too fast. He faced Mordak. Mordak also held a rock.

Mordak's hair was almost all gray and wispy. His fingers seemed long but that was only because his hands had become so thin. He eyed Kelsey warily.

Kelsey eyed him back.

They circled slowly under the impossible sky. They were close enough to throw their rocks at each other. They circled.

Mordak projected across the distance to him in a hissing, breathy language. "Kelsey. Are you willing to listen at the moment?"

Kelsey eyed him.

"There may come times when these words will give you solace," Mordak went on.

"What words?" Kelsey shouted back and he sounded angrier than he'd intended to. He did not like having his moment of happiness interrupted for this.

"I've forgiven you your wrongs. I understand them."

"You've forgiven *me*?"

"Indeed. And some day you will do the same for me. No matter how unlikely it may seem at times."

"Alright, Mister. Look--"

"No. You. Listen. Remember this moment when you sit among the poppies. Now, I believe I have an appointment with you near an Oak where, I expect, things will become suddenly quite clear to me."

"What is it with you and this Oak?"

But old Mordak was already falling away from him.

****

A black sky held one bright point, too small to be a sun, too bright to be a moon. Bundled in heavy coats a group of people huddled at the edge of a crystalline bank. A young woman struggled in the water below. Her coats bound her and she did not seam to know how to swim at all. Kelsey stripped off a heavy layer and dove in to rescue her.

The icy water shocked his skin and his pulse sky-rocketed, but he managed to grab the struggling lady from behind and pull her close enough to shore to be pulled out by her friends.

The strange, bundled folk pulled Kelsey out as well and then, stripping off the woman's wrappings and offering her dry ones of their own, they led her off leaving Kelsey to shiver in the icy waste.

He tried to stand, to follow them, but the shiver had reached his bones and he could not support his own weight. He fell backward but the world did not recede. He lay on his back in the soft, cold crystals. His feet were numb, he noticed, and he was glad. They were less cold that way.

Then he wasn't cold at all. He felt warm all over. He began to unclasp his jacket. It was difficult with his stiff, unfeeling fingers, but he managed. He was sweating. It occurred to him that this was probably odd, that it might mean something bad, that he was freezing to death. With effort he managed to pull another layer of his clothing away from his shoulders and lay back again.

Salia fell to his side. She was very young. She was very beautiful. She immediately set upon him and covered him in kisses and hugs.

"You're alright! Oh, god. Kelsey I thought-- I saw-- I'm so glad you're okay!"

"I'm a little warm."

"Warm? What? Oh boy. I've got to get you into some clothes."

And as Salia wrapped him in her own outer layer of clothing he faded into unconsciousness.

****

Waking, he knew he was in a warmer place. He knew he was not dead. Remembering, he shivered at sensations retriggered. He shivered at his nearness to death.

He twitched a little when he tried to move and chuckled at his own stiffness. Working his muscles more slowly, he came to his feet.

Mordak watched him. He wore his long, thick, gray hair proudly and he smiled. On the balls of his feet, ready to move, Mordak gripped a seven inch steel rod with a richly jeweled handle.

Kelsey found a similar weapon strapped to his calf. It occurred to him to reach for it, but bending seemed like a bad idea, just now.

"I assume we're going to fight again...?" Mordak asked, easily.

"Do we have to?" Kelsey asked, stiff and trying not to appear weak.

Mordak curled down the edges of his mouth, thinking and shook his head. "No. No, we don't. It wouldn't do us much good anyway."

"Alright, then."

"Alright." And Mordak backed off a few feet, then, before he turned, "Every now and then, we really are heroes, you and I." He smiled and bowed his head for a moment with a cap-tipping flourish of a gesture that might have been intended to mock Kelsey. He walked off, joining a crowd of pedestrians.

There was a good swagger in Mordak's walk. He walked like a man who worked hard and enjoyed his work.

Kelsey felt the increased distance between himself and the world around him as he mused.

****

The forest burned. The treetops danced with flames. The underbrush smoldered, giving off thick smoke. Animals shot by, escaping the blaze.

A fallen and burning tree pinned Salia's legs. His stiffness was unimportant. He had to save Salia.

He tried lifting the log but it was far too heavy and he was far too weak. He located a long, strong bough and, leaning back against it found the leverage to free Salia. Her legs were not broken, though they were badly bruised and cut in places.

She struggled to speak but she was tired and in shock. He carried her through the wood until he came to a stream where he knew he could protect her if the fire blew this way, though from the crackling sounds it seemed to be receding.

He took her head in his lap and stroked her long gray hair as she slept. When her sleep was deep and her breathing steady he set about cleaning her injuries.

Finding a crossbow strapped to his back, he sat guard. He listened to the trickling of the stream. He watched bright, close-set stars decorate the sky.

Salia woke for a time, but she did not speak. She lay there, gray and tired, and watched her young hero guarding her. It was the first time in a long while that she had felt safe.

Mordak fell to him then, aiming a crossbow of his own. Kelsey struggled to draw back his dart. As he tried to figure the mechanism he heard a soft *thung* and looked up sharply.

Salia had moved swiftly. She had thrown herself into the path of trajectory and taken the dart for him. Mordak, enraged, screamed at her as he fell away. "You bitch. That would have gotten him! I could have--" and he was gone, falling into an impossible distance.

Kelsey was at her side at once. She did not stir. She did not breath. He found no pulse at her veined wrist. He cradled her again and pressed her wrinkled hand to his cheek and wept.

"Oh, Salia," he said. "I tried to protect you. I really loved you. God I wish I'd had a chance to tell you. God I wish--"

As he fell he wondered if her body would fall too or if the game, for her, had come to a true end.

****

VI

Where the crossbow had been, now there was a long bow. Where there had been a forest, now there was a town.

A woman crouched, straining. Tears streamed from her eyes. Her hands clenched and stretched, clenched and stretched. She cried out. Kelsey moved to the woman's side and took her hand.

"You should lie down," he said. "Let me help you."

"No." She said. "My water's broken. I can't lie down now."

This seemed odd to Kelsey, but he helped her through it as best he could.

Passersby ignored them. A baby was born in that place. It had all its fingers and toes, and all its features were in the right places. It began to cry and Kelsey did too.

Dazed and exhausted, Kelsey stumbled to an Inn and ordered himself an ale. He sat with his back to the wall and turned a pewter stein between his fingers.

He watched the pedestrians on the street beyond the window. He thought it was a figment of his imagination but when he looked again she was still there.

He ran from the Inn and grabbed Salia from behind. His third full stein was still gripped in his left hand. He turned her to him and kissed her full upon on the lips.

Her hair was beautiful. Her eyes gleamed.

"You again!" she said, delighted.

"Oh, God. Salia, I love you."

"But we hardly know each other, Kelsey." She kissed him back.

"You-- I--" finding no way to tell her what had happened he let the thought go unspoken. "Come on. I've found an Inn."

And he led her across the street. He never made it back to the Inn.

****

Mordak attacked him violently on a field laden with goldenrod. Kelsey defended himself.

****

Mordak attacked him with a knife in an alley way. He screamed accusations at him while they fought, but Kelsey could make no sense of the man's words. He fought until he was very tired. Then he fell.

****

In a wooden shack Kelsey found a bed with a mattress that was much too thin. He lay down and wrote in his journal for a time, trying to make sense of his most recent Falls. He shut his eyes then. Though he felt weary he was not yet able to sleep.

A soft rain began to fall. It pattered on the shack's tin roof. He listened to the sound and waited to hear an explosion, a scream, a gun shot.

The door creaked open.

Kelsey rolled out of the bed.

The visitor was Salia. She smiled. "Kelsey!" She said. "It seems like forever."

"Good to see you, Sal."

"I was beginning to think I'd never get this back to you." She held out a journal almost identical to the one in which he'd been writing. It differed only in seeming a little more time worn and battered.

He lifted his own journal and examined it.

"Oh," she said. "I guess you don't need it yet."

"I haven't come up with any kind of a job here, yet. You know anything about this place?"

"I don't think you've ever mentioned it."

Thunder cracked. Lightning flashed through the sky. Salia flinched at the sound. Another sound came through the storm, a sound that was not weather related, a sound they'd both come to know all too well. They ran together through the rain toward the screams. They had heroing to do.

****

Wind whipped at Kelsey's hair. It pressed his clothing against his body. The tail ends of his long jacket waved behind him.

The rocky terrain impeded his progress, but it didn't matter as he had no real destination.

He reached the horizon, the edge, the very lip of the world. Looking out on the stars beneath and around him he was overcome with dizziness and vertigo. He stepped away from the edge.

Salia's arms wrapped around him. Her lips touched his. He turned from the edge and gave to the kiss. It lasted for a long, long time.

When their lips parted at last, Kelsey saw that Salia was very young. Her skin was smooth and her hair soft in the bright starlight.

"I'm liking this Game more and more," she said.

Her breath warmed a little place on his neck and he said, "It has its moments."

They kissed some more then. Kelsey was surprised to find that the star-scape had changed dramatically when the kiss ended, not as with a Fall but rather as though much time had lapsed and the night had worn on as he had lost himself entirely in the exploration of Salia's soft lips.

"You look pretty young," Kelsey said. "You probably have a lot of questions."

"You told me I'll always have questions. You said that answers are never as important as action."

"I did?"

"Let's make love again."

"Again? But you were a lot older when..." She nibbled at his ear and he stopped trying to figure it all out.

Gravel and pebbles made for a less than ideal playing surface, but that in no way diminished the quality of the athletic performances. Heroes on a break, they made love with all the vigor and commitment they routinely put to saving lives. *If this,* he thought, *is all the reward I get for what I do, the work is worth it.*

"My hero," Salia muttered softly and crinkled up her eyes, waiting to be kissed some more.

"My heroine," he replied and made the waiting come to an end.

****

VII

The tents of the tribesman kept out the rain well at night. It worried Kelsey that he had learned this twice, now. He had not, since last paying rent in Manhattan, slept in the same bed twice.

Not that the pile of wooly pelts he slept on could be called a bed, but they were soft and warm and pleasant and twice they had been there when he awoke. All he had wanted, of course, was for the Game to come to an end; but for it to end here, amongst these foul smelling people? That would not do.

What if, somehow, he was here for good? There seemed to be no threat here, no sign of Salia or of Mordak.

The Kaerem had welcomed him into their small community, and when he had shown them the technique of cooking under the coals they truly began to trust him and offered him the well-pelted sleeping assignment.

The rainy nights ran long. On occasion, the steady patter would cease. Kelsey woke with a start at one of these claps of silence and stepped out of the tent to see a few tribesman, also out, catching a fleeting glimpse of their star field through the brief break in the cloud cover.

A fire always burned in the center of the camp. Three men tended it during the day and another three at night. These six were held in high regard and were said to give wise counsel. Kelsey went to them. He had to speak with someone.

"Hello, Kelsey Darson," said one of the Tenders.

"Hi," Kelsey said, then didn't know how to ask.

"I'm afraid we don't have time for idle chat today, Kelsey. Ill breezes have been rising."

"I have a question."

The man nodded a willingness to hear him out.

"How long do you think I'll be staying here?" but he wasn't satisfied with the question.

"Until you have done what you are here to do. Is that not so for us all?"

Kelsey decided that those who are supposedly sage are the same in any world. He shook his head, then said, "What ill breezes?"

"There is a tribe to the north. A large one. They wish to have what belongs to us."

"What belongs to us?"

"We have some things, our little tribe. Some things that are hard to come by." He added, "They will attack after dusk and before dawn."

"I will fight with you. For you."

The Tenders exchanged looks and all nodded at once. Kelsey decided to sleep through the day to be ready for a night attack.

He awoke, again amongst the pelts, to the sounds of action. The thudding of the tribesmen's feet upon the hard ground was a constant along with the beginning of the night's precipitation.

He stepped out into the drizzle donning an animal skull helmet and tying his loin cloth a little tighter than usual just to insure that it would not slip and distract him. He wore a long knife strapped in a sheath to his left leg.

The setting sun still showed angry red at the horizon. All about the camp men made provisions. Most wore helmets of bone or wood. All carried weapons. The sense of imminent danger filled the air. Kelsey headed for the fire. He realized that it was nice to walk to a place knowing where he was headed for a change. As alien as he was in his surroundings, he had come to like many of the tribesmen, to enjoy their company, to consider a few of them his friends. He could come to accept this life, this place as his home.

Seeing that the Tenders had left their usual post he suddenly felt the fear which gripped those about him. The fact of the untended fire made clear to him the significance of the impending attack.

At a flicker of movement he turned to find that Salia walked with him. "You know what the job is, yet?" She asked.

"We're here to fend off an attacking army. It looks like it's going to be one hell of a battle."

"Ah," she said, and looked a little sad and quite tired.

"Cheer up. There'll be lots of bad guys to fight. Come on."

At this she smiled. She almost laughed. "Bad guys. Alright. I can do this."

"Like we have a choice."

A long spear, like a shaft released from giant's bow, whistled through the air and stuck into the ground.

"Here we go," Kelsey said. The attackers came over the ridge crest. The battle began.

As battles will, it raged. Through the night, through three or four pauses in the eternal downpour, Kelsey fought with his knife. Occasionally opportunities arose to make use of better weapons which, in the course of events, came into his hands. The thrill of the melee took him away from himself for a time and he was grateful for it. The battle was loud, the issues were clear and Salia was alive, fighting beside him.

When it became clear that a clean defense was impossible, the tents and belongings of the camp were moved away by the women and those children who were old enough and strong enough to help. The Tenders who had taken up arms and joined the battle fell back as well. They brought the coals from the fire pit in a specially treated wooden box which was blackened and scarred on the inside. Once the camp was well away and safely set Kelsey and the tribesmen retreated leaving the somewhat eroded attacking army to put together a new plan.

When the tribe had reassembled Salia was gone. One of the Tenders, not the one with whom he'd spoken earlier, took Kelsey aside and gave him a small, capped bottle. It was carved of ivory white horn. "Kelsey Darson, you have done much for us this day. Though you are not of our blood you fought for us and with us and perhaps you have spared the shedding of some of that blood which you do not share. Take this with you. It is an antidote for any poison and if it is swallowed while a man still lives, that man's wounds shall heal and any sickness leave his body. For those lives you have saved here, perhaps we can save yours in some day to come, eh?"

Though Kelsey was skeptical about the potion's effectiveness he accepted it, thanking the man. As he spoke he felt a little removed from his words as though he was merely projecting a façade. Despite the bonds he had developed to this place, he felt quite alone and apart.

****

Kelsey Darson muttered his name to himself, reminding himself of his identity as he got his bearings. He leaned against the tree to his right and examined the bark of the one to his left. It was iridescent, seeming both green and red. It was very smooth, like porcelain.

Salia walked along the ridge to the north and he shouted to her, calling her name.

She shouted back without slowing. "Have you seen him?"

"Who?"

"Mordak! Have you seen the bastard?"

"What? No. Wait up!"

"No time, Kelsey. Go away. I'm busy. I don't want to talk."

"What? What did I do?"

"Nothing," she shouted and the word was biting somehow. "You didn't do anything."

The whinny of an animal that might have been a distant relative of the horse spun him around. The creature's rider lay on the ground in a crumpled heap as the beast trotted off. Kelsey ran to the man and resuscitated him.

When the man coughed and came to, Salia had fallen or walked beyond the horizon.

<u>VIII</u>

Under a bright, bright sky Kelsey watched the figures below him on the obsidian plane. Mordak he recognized, but he had never seen the woman with whom Mordak walked. She had long black hair and it danced in the gusty winds. They walked together well. They looked good. They looked like a couple.

"Mordak!" he cried.

Mordak turned, looking up, locating him on the bluff, but already that world was receding and Mordak and his lover with it.

****

The grasses rose high enough to impede Kelsey's progress. He beat them aside with his long staff and made his slow way across the field.

A sharp rustling to his right stopped him, drew his attention. He listened.

Mordak broke through the cover onto the path Kelsey had just cut. There were dark bags beneath his eyes and fire in them. He did not speak, though a guttural sound came from him as he swung the staff, charging.

Kelsey blocked the blow and returned it. He fought hard, doing a good deal more than defending himself. He studied Mordak as he fought. He had never seen the man so animal. There were no questions now, no accusations, no rantings. Just rage and blood-thirst.

Kelsey fell back at the attack, pressing through the grass, pushing forward when he could. He neither shed nor drew blood before he fell.

****

Mordak was even more enraged in the next place. He screamed as he swung wildly with his club and there was nothing Kelsey could do except back away and hope his foe would tire.

Eventually Mordak fell away, still howling, and vanished.

Kelsey let out a long sigh as he vanished himself.

****

A lightning storm dropped angry flashes over a tightly built city. The streets were narrow and the proportions of the storm magnificent.

Buildings shattered at the electrical onslaught and, though Kelsey saw Salia once lugging an elderly woman in a fireman's carry, he was far too involved in his own business to go make conversation.

An old man called for help in half-coherent phrases. Digging through the rubble, Kelsey found a cement stairway running down into the earth. He descended the steps, shouting words of comfort and following the voice. He found the man half buried in dust and broken plaster.

In the process of freeing the man, he was aware of the journal falling from his pocket. He made a mental note to retrieve it before he was done here.

The man was bruised and bleeding but nothing was broken and, with some help, he could walk. Kelsey helped him up the stairs. Then, hearing the hysterical screams of a woman, he ran off to continue his work.

Some time later he remembered the journal and hoped he would have the time to find the collapsed building in which it had been lost.

****

IX

Those sweet breezes thrilled Kelsey just as they had the first time, stirring the warm, silent water of the pond. He let Salia sleep, and sat near her, watching, even though he did not expect a threat to come to her. It was nice to see her sleep, to know she was safe, to feel he was safe.

The silk smooth skin of her face flinched at some dreamed danger, but the moment passed and again she looked blissful. Kelsey found that he was smiling a little.

At least an hour had passed when she stirred and sat up. She sucked in the air happily.

"Good morning," Kelsey said.

"Good morning," she replied brightly. "What a great place."

"You've never seen it before?"

She shook her head. "You know what the job is, here?"

Kelsey filled her in on the wonder and nature of this place. Knowing she would be here again, she took a long look around, soaking in the sights of the place. Then she rejoined him by the water and put her arms around him. She held him that way for a long time, not speaking, not kissing.

"Is something wrong?" Kelsey asked.

"I don't think I like this Game, Kelsey," she said. "I really think I hate it."

"Me too," he said. "Anything in particular you're thinking of?"

"I saw... I'm pretty sure I saw..." and she trailed off.

"You saw me die," he guessed. "Didn't you?"

She nodded her head. "It was--"

"Don't tell me," he said. Then, "I love you."

"I love you, too, Kelsey. I never got to tell you that."

"You got to tell me," he said. "You're telling me now. And some day, when I die, and you watch, I'll remember it and I'll know. Okay?"

She sniffled a little, and nodded again, kissing his neck. "You smell good," she said, "like smoke and leather."

"You smell good, too," he lied and enjoyed her kisses and her touch and her body.

****

<u>X</u>

The hood of his cloak made Kelsey's cheeks itch. He pushed it back and made his way down the long corridor. At the end of the hall a door of mahogany panels swung easily open at his touch. He stepped through into a spacious chamber. The air was cool and every sound echoed against the marble walls and floor.

He listened to the sound as his heels clacked on the hard surface.

A sharp sound came from beyond a door at the far side of the chamber. It might have been a startled dog. It might not.

He went to and passed through that door. A dagger in an ornate scabbard adorned his chest like jewelry. The small horn bottle still hung from its cord about his neck, under his shirt. He checked for his journal as a matter of habit before remembering, once again, that he had lost it.

The door led to another hallway, this one narrower and less well lit. The continuing sounds of muffled struggle led him to a room that was locked. He pounded for entry, but the sounds of struggle did not pause. "What's going on in there?" he shouted.

"Hi, Kelsey," Mordak's voice came back to him.

Now he threw his shoulder against the door heavily. It moved a little against the drop lock, but did not swing. He smashed at it again. He heard a whimper from inside. He also heard a slight crack at the impact. He took a steep back and, with enough force to bruise himself badly, hurled his body weight against the wood.

The crossbar gave way with a heavy snap and the door came open. There was a brief flicker of movement that may have been Mordak's disappearance.

Kelsey was alone in the room with Salia. He moved to her at once and untied her hands. He took the gag from her mouth and, because she was shaking, he moved to hold her. She pulled away sharply and covered herself as well as she could with her tattered clothes.

"Don't touch me," she said. He had never seen her so shaken, so frightened. He wanted to comfort her.

"Are you alright?"

"I'm fine," she snapped. "Just leave me alone. Is there a bath around here? I have to take a bath."

"Are you're sure you're okay, Salia? Do you need--"

"I'm fine. Kelsey, I'm fine. Okay? Can you just accept that? Can't you just accept that?"

Kelsey wanted to hold her. He wanted to stroke her cheek. He wanted to make it all better.

But it was hard with so much distance between himself and the world around him.

****

Mordak grinned, his sabre drawn and ready. His hair was very gray but still thick. It draped long over shoulders. His jewelled hilt gleamed in the sunlight.

Kelsey had felt the weight of his sword in his hand before the world around him even came into full focus. He had seen the grin while it was still a distant speck in the darkness between worlds. And from the time he had seen it he had not fallen, he had dived. The Fall was driven by his rage. The pressure he applied to push the place into focus caused his arrival to become a sharp thing, painful through his chest and shoulders.

He howled at the sharpness of the landing and he lunged, hard and fast.

"You prick!" he screamed at the man. "You think I don't know what you did in that room? You son of a -- " He cut himself off, saving his breath for the fight.

Calmly, almost disinterestedly, Mordak backed away, parrying. Kelsey pressed forward, only vaguely aware of the cobblestones beneath his feet but never losing his step. Mordak, with infuriating ease, staved off each cut, backing away smoothly.

It seemed Mordak was suddenly backing away much more swiftly. And he was taking the world with him.

****

The sky did not matter. The terrain did not matter. The weapon was a heavy ball on a short rope and the figure on the horizon was Mordak. Far off, yes, but Kelsey recognized the gait, the body shape.

His eyes locked on that figure and he walked with the sun burning above him and, after a time, to his right. Slowly, slowly, the figure grew and as soon as he was near enough, Kelsey hurled his weapon.

The ball arced in the air and Kelsey fell.

****

Kelsey attacked Mordak by a bright clear ocean. Mordak defended himself.

Kelsey tried to curse him but his words sounded like gibberish to his own ears and he could not imagine how they sounded to the young object of his rage.

Mordak's defense was clumsy and untaught. Had he not fallen away just then, Kelsey was certain he'd have had him.

****

Kelsey started off toward the pub across the street. A carriage drawn by a team of goats trampled by. A big, bald, tattooed man loomed over a frightened looking young woman at the corner. Kelsey did not move to offer her his assistance.

Salia called to him but he pretended not to hear her. He did not care how young or old she was, or where she came in from. He had failed to protect her. She was the one thing he cherished in this game and he had let Mordak hurt her -- hell, he'd let Mordak kill her, but that hadn't been as bad. What Mordak had done to her while she lived, that was the worst of it. He remembered her pulling away from him. He remembered falling away from her, unable to offer comfort or solace. He could not turn at her voice. He could not look into her eyes.

He wanted a little ale and Mordak's head. That was all. Mordak, for no reason, had sought to destroy him and systematically to destroy those things in the Game that brought him the most happiness. He would not get away with it.

****

The sun beat upon Kelsey's neck as he walked in toward the city, hoping to find Mordak.

Salia fell to his side and did not speak at once. Kelsey did not look at her. She walked with him and examined his profile, the set of his jaw. At last she said, "Are you okay, Kelsey?"

He thought of answers he might give, but when he contemplated giving voice his throat caught and he feared he might cry. He kept silent. He maintained the set of his jaw.

"Are you angry with me, Kelsey? Did I do something?" She paused, waiting, walking, then, "Is there something I'm going to do?"

Still he did not answer. He walked. He hoped that she could not see the tears welling.

"Is it alright if I walk with you a while?"

They walked. He heard her begin to sniffle, walking beside him. He stopped. He tried once more to find words he could speak without crying. For a moment, he felt he might be able to as he had become quite emotionally removed, distant . . .

****

<u>XI</u>

The window looked out over the bright lights of a neon and halogen city. Kelsey paid the city below little mind. He did not examine the food left on the table before him. The design of his chair made no difference to him.

He checked for a weapon and found only a small pill-box Velcroed to his hip. Reflected in the window glass he had already located Mordak just two tables away, tasting wine.

Feigning a bloody nose, Kelsey held his napkin over his face and rushed past Mordak's table, dropping two tablets into his victim's glass as he moved. If poison was the weapon of the realm, so be it.

He continued moving and, reaching the exit, stopped to look back. Mordak clutched at his belly. He appeared to be middle aged. His jaw line was visibly fading to blue, then he vanished as if with great distance.

Kelsey vanished in similar fashion, feeling unsatisfied. He had still not seen Mordak die. He could not be certain...

****

The screams of the dying meant nothing to Kelsey, now. He walked through disasters, battles and catastrophes seeking Mordak, hoping to find his body, huddled, clutching its belly in death. He did not know how long this search went on. Falling became as much a part of the search as walking.

****

When Kelsey next found Mordak he was in a strange, urban environment. Kelsey wore no weapon save his gloves which had claw-like spikes protruding from the striking surface of the knuckles.

Mordak was very young, not dead at all. His gloves were designed with rough metal plates. Kelsey grasped the opportunity and called out Mordak's name. Mordak looked at him.

"You know my name?" the young man asked.

"I know you, Mordak. I know your future. Too bad you're not going to get to see it."

With a quick grab he took Mordak by the shoulder and drew back his hand for a skull piercing blow but his hand seemed to keep pulling back, taking him with it, away from the world, from the moment of opportunity, from the light.

****

In the next place Mordak was somewhat older and he lay with a young woman as Kelsey fell to him. The woman had long dark hair, and Mordak, lost in the feel and smell of it, was unaware of Kelsey's arrival for a moment.

This gave the bitter hero time to savor the drawing of his shiv. He set himself for his strike, let his muscles tense, then pushed the blade forward with his weight behind it.

The movement made a sound against the floor boards. The girl looked up, putting herself in the path of Kelsey's blade. He felt it enter her soft flesh and continue through something somewhat less soft.

"Damn you!" he heard himself scream in a rough, nasal tongue and he pulled back the narrow blade knowing he could not undo the act.

"Damn *you*!" Mordak yelled back, moving to cradle the woman as the room fell away from Kelsey.

****

Kelsey attacked Mordak on a rocky slope.

****

Kelsey attacked Mordak under a sky filled with moons. The rage in Mordak's eyes mirrored the rage in his own. Sparks leaped from the machete blades in the colorful darkness.

****

Just a few hundred yards away was an Oak Tree. Kelsey felt the tree was important, though he couldn't say why. *Perhaps*, he thought, *Salia mentioned it.* He wondered if there was something he was supposed to remember to do, here. He walked toward the tree, hoping to remember.

He circled the bole of the tree at a distance and discovered Mordak. The old man sat, cross-legged, in the shade of the tree on the far side. His long, wispy hair fluttered in the easy wind.

Kelsey's hand found a hilt and drew a weapon. It was a long, wire-thin blade with a wooden grip. He lunged at Mordak and, rather than standing to defend himself, rather than rolling to avoid the thrust, Mordak smiled.

So slender was the blade that it seemed to meet no resistance as it pierced flesh, muscle and bone. No blood spilled as Mordak's heart was pierced. The man smiled a little.

"Well, Kelsey. There it is." he said and he twitched in pain. "Was it good for you?"

And he slumped and lay still.

Kelsey could see that he was not breathing. He waited to fall, wearing an idiotic victory grin.

It did not happen, the Fall. The air was still. The body of Mordak was too, his bony fingers slightly curved. The Oak tree made no sound.

Kelsey sat down. He examined the features of his dead adversary. He thought back on the time, the energy he'd put in to see this man dead. Now the man was dead. Very old, then dead.

He reached for his journal, then remembered that he had lost it.

At last a breeze stirred. Kelsey turned to face into it, tired, drained. At last his rage abated. He hoped Salia would forgive him for his rudeness when he saw her again.

He looked at Mordak again, at the proud lines of his still features. "Game's over Mordak," he said. Then, "You brought it on yourself, you know." He looked away. "I never wanted to fight in the first place."

****

Kelsey bellied to the bar and asked for an ale. Everything went soft and mushy. The floor came up to meet him.

He rode waves of confusing darkness, struggling toward a far off light. His body snapped as his consciousness returned, and he found he was on his back. Mordak loomed over him, angry, middle aged and holding a ram's horn flask. There was a little blood on the flask.

Kelsey touched the back of his head and his hand came away wet. He struggled to his feet. Before he could stand, Mordak began to throw another punch. Kelsey fell back to avoid the blow and kept falling.

Why -- and in his Fall his thoughts echoed in his mind like a herd of voices -- *must I always be an idiot?*

****

Even as he fell, Kelsey had a sense of what this next place would bring. Thinking this, he wondered if he was, perhaps, becoming conscious of some previously subconscious form of control over his Falls. He determined to put into distinct images the sense that he had . . .

But thinking this he realized he was dreading what he sensed. Perhaps he could redirect himself if he just . . .

The point of light was coming up fast. Trying to hold back, trying to give himself time to put together the fragmented images, he turned his landing into an electrical jolt and a body slam that left him with a deep stiffness in his back.

He knew he had just had an important thought of some sort but it was all gone . . . like the reflections of a dream shattered by the painful pitch of consciousness.

Glass and steel made him think of home, but the smells were unfamiliar. The smells were like those in that place, long ago, with the tall buildings. The buildings here were not so tall.

He remembered meeting Salia. He walked amongst the buildings, hoping to find her, not really expecting to. He remembered the razor she'd brought him, then. He felt at the hem of his short jacket. There was an odd lump. He couldn't see a way to pull it out without damaging the jacket. He reached into his pocket and found that its inside lining was torn a little. He worked his fingers through the hole and fished from the hidden interior something that felt like a rounded, lumpy ball of clay.

Green clay, he learned. He rolled it on his arm and, with a slightly painful pulling sensation, it took away the hair. He found a building with blackened windows and headed for it.

The glass gave him a startling view of himself. His beard was quite thick and far longer than he'd guessed. Streaks of gray had made a home in it. Gray had also begun to make bright inroads at his temples with flecks already appearing on his crown. He tried to gauge how much time had passed since that place with the tall buildings. He could not.

He rolled the ball of shaving clay on his beard until he could see the skin of his face again. Lines lived at the corners of his eyes and his throat seemed leathery.

Mordak appeared behind him and a little to the right.

Kelsey turned swiftly enough to have his weapon drawn and raised in defense before Mordak's first assault came. Beyond his rage, realizing he was a good deal older than the man who attacked him, Kelsey defended himself easily. The battle seemed effortless, even pleasant. He knew he would not win. Mordak could not die this young. He knew he would not lose. He had not yet bawled like a baby by the pond. So he enjoyed the fight for the fight's sake and knew that his distracted smile could only serve to further enrage Mordak.

****

XII

The frozen lake was like a pane of glass. Kelsey could only see a shoreline in one direction, so he made for it. Layer upon layer of clothing made it difficult to walk and the going was slow on the slippery surface. He lost his footing more than once.

There was no break in the snowy whiteness along the shoreline. Then, at once, there was. A figure appeared and walked along the edge of the lake. It might have been Salia. Speeding up he slipped and thudded heavily on the hard ice.

He let out a sound on impact. The figure noticed him now and called out. "You!" she shouted.

Carefully planting each foot and shifting his weight with conscious deliberation, he made his way toward her. She moved toward him in similarly awkward fashion. He saw that her hair was dark. He had seen her before, but his memory could not place where. He wondered if she was someone he had known in New York.

"I have questions to ask you," she said.

"Oh?" he asked.

"What's your problem? What have you got against Mordak?"

Kelsey smiled lightly and shook his head with some little sadness. "Nothing. Against Mordak? Right now, nothing."

"Why do you keep attacking him?"

"I'm done attacking him," Kelsey told her. "Now the attacks come from him."

"You promise?"

"Any attack I make on him from now on is all in the past. I promise."

The woman furrowed her brow trying to put together the tenses of his statement. "I love him," she said. "I'll do whatever I have to to protect him." There was the edge of a threat in her voice.

"I know," Kelsey told her, and he did. He remembered her now, remembered killing her. He looked away. "What's your name?"

"Chryslas. And yours?"

"Darson. Kelsey Darson."

He wanted to ask her questions and answer any that she had, but he felt quite removed from the conversation.

****

There was a bounce in Salia's walk, and her hair was silkier than Kelsey could ever remember having seen it. He watched her, enjoying the grace of her movements, the line of her body, just for a moment before calling out to her.

When he did call her name she stopped in her tracks and turned slowly to face him. Without nearing him, she studied his features. "You know my name," she said.

"Of course I do, Salia. You--" and then, seeing the confusion in her face he said, "Have you never met me?"

"Never." She said it with certainty.

"Come on," he said, "I'll explain this to you as best I can."

She walked with him in the direction he chose, but she kept a little distance between them and it made Kelsey uncomfortable. This was Salia. How could she be so distrustful of him? He remembered the times he had failed her, allowing her to be killed and later to be raped. Perhaps, he decided, she is right to distrust me.

He told her of the nature of their meetings, of the non-linear nature of their shared travels. She did not understand. As he tried to explain the Game there was a sudden, sharp whistling sound from the sky above and a plummeting meteorite slammed into a farm house.

"I have to go help those people," Salia said.

"Forget it. You should understand this. The stuff I'm explaining to you. It will make things easier in the long --"

"Look, Darson. People are going to die in there if I don't go help them. Got it?" And with that she turned and jogged away from him toward the building.

****

Mordak came at Kelsey Darson hard and fast. The double bladed weapon hummed as it cut the air and Kelsey's hummed in response as he defended himself. Kelsey listened to the harmonies and clangs as he fought.

One of the singing blades caught his upper arm and blood flowed, dripping down his wrist, making his grip damp and slippery.

"Got you, Bastard!" Mordak yelled.

"And I've got you, Mordak. Give it up. It's pointless. Neither of us is going to win. Not now. Not today. Not 'til you get to the Oak tree. Then I'll win. And I guess you will too, in a way."

"What the hell is that supposed to--?"

****

Mordak attacked on a small, sandy island. He was furious, blithering. Kelsey had killed the only woman he had ever loved, his only companion in the game.

Mordak screamed of revenge and swore he would have it.

Kelsey defended himself.

****

Kelsey defended the caves that had been cut into the cliff face. Salia came to his side as he fought.

"Have you seen Mordak?" she asked.

"Not here," he told her.

"I have to find him. The bastard raped me, Kelse."

"I know." He cut free a long ladder and let it fall taking a number of the invaders with it. "I tried to get in. To stop him."

"I know," Salia said. Then, "If you see him, kill him."

"Is that a Buddha joke?"

"What?"

"Never mind. You want to give me a hand here?"

"I have to find Mordak." She turned away and began to walk.

He ran to catch her. "I've already killed him," he told her. "I hunted him down until I killed him."

She looked at him, looked into his eyes. "Really?"

"Really."

"Well," she said. "It's over then."

"Not really," he told her. "Not ever, I don't think."

Salia nodded, only half understanding. She was hurt, wounded, deep in her psyche. Kelsey could see that she was not thinking clearly.

****

XIII

The pond stirred as it always had before with sweet and gentle breezes. The trees shished their leaves together as if to greet him. "Hi guys," Kelsey said to them.

There was a splash and a disturbance in the water. Kelsey could not, at once, see what had cause the noise, but after a moment Salia surfaced. Her gray hair was wet and tangled. She swam to shore and climbed out, dripping.

She moved to Kelsey's side. He could not remember her being this old except . . . once. He did not have words so Salia broke the silence.

"I'm old, aren't I?"

He nodded.

"It's ages since I've seen a mirror."

"That happens," he said. Then, "You're still beautiful."

"Why thank you, kind sir," she said. Then, "So are you."

He smiled.

"So," she prompted him. When he did not respond, "Why won't you look at me?"

"I've seen-- I've seen so much, now. More than I'd ever--"

She touched his cheek with her hand. "It's okay. So have I."

He took a deep breath, sucking in the sweetness of the air, the smells that had come to mean 'home' more than street-vended chestnuts or urine in the subway.

"How do I die, Kelsey? I know it happens soon. How does it come about?"

"Too soon," he told her. "Way too soon. There were so many things I wished I'd told you."

"Tell me now," she said. "What did you want me to know?"

Now he did turn to her. Her eyes were still bright and without sadness. The creases were deep from a lifetime of flinching at explosions and gunshots and lightning strikes. "I love you," he told her. "I've always loved you. I'll always love you. And I thank you for-- for getting me through at the beginning. And for sharing the Game with me. And for your smile, and your -- "

He did not fall away. She took his face in her hands and drew him into a kiss. Then she told him the truth. "I think this is good bye for me, Kelsey. I've always loved you too. From that very first time. Even then. When I didn't know if I should trust you."

"I'm sorry I let you down, Salia. I really am."

"Don't be," she told him. "You've made my whole life worth living." And she kissed him again.

Kelsey had never made love to such an old woman before. It was almost exactly the same as making love to a young woman or a middle aged woman. It was beautiful and soft and sweeter than the breezes that caressed them.

They lay together then, in the afterglow. After a while Salia said, "You seem so far away."

"I do?" he asked.
"Goodbye, Kelsey. I love -- "
And she shrank away as if with sudden distance.

****

XIV

The angry wind pushed against Kelsey as he walked so he turned around and let it push him from behind.

High clouds rolled through the sky very fast. He heard the harsh voice of Mordak calling to him and turned to face the young man's rage once again.

He fought now with no real interest. He did not hate his old enemy any more. All Mordak wanted was revenge, and rightly so. Kelsey had killed his lover, the one person who might have made Mordak's life worth living. As he ducked and jabbed he hoped he would have a chance to tell him that some day, to tell him he did not hate, to tell him he was forgiven for killing Salia, even for raping her.

Perhaps if he could tell him when he was young enough, before it had all begun, he could change the events, make the thing come out differently. Perhaps they could be friends next time around, heroes together. It was worth a shot.

Kelsey landed a lucky blow and Mordak fell and kept on falling.

****

In a cavern lit by florescent fungus, Kelsey made out a far off dripping of water. He made a direction as best he could and headed that way. The sound diminished and he reversed direction.

After a few steps he heard a third sound, a shuffling beyond the dripping and his own foot falls. He stopped, straining his ears. "Salia?" he shouted. "Mordak?"

"Kelsey?" Salia's voice came back to him. "Where are you?"

"I have no idea." He shouted back. "You?"

"By a pool. Can you hear the water dripping?"

"I'm already on my way. Stay put."

"I think I'm falling, Kelsey. I'll leave your -- " and her voice dopplered away to silence.

When he found the pool Salia was not there. His journal lay beside the still water. He smiled when he saw it and stooped to pick it up. He did not know how she had come to have it. He had lost it in crisis. He had not given to her. He looked through it. It ended where he had last written in it. He kissed it once and ran his fingers over the battered leather. He sat down, planning to write in it, but he had no time.

****

The ground shook continuously, not violently but steadily. Cracks appeared in the concrete pavement. The thump and rumble of collapsing buildings filled the air.

Kelsey shifted direction heading for the sound of the screams. He stopped short, startled by Mordak's landing. He drew his weapon. Mordak eyed him warily.

"Are we going to fight, Kelsey? Or do you think we can save some lives, here?" Mordak's hair was dark, his skin smooth.

"Let's be heroes."

Side by side they pulled survivors free.

****

Kelsey guarded Salia as she slept, young, under the tent of a weeping willow's long branches.

He remained alert the entire time, but he rested against the tree's trunk. His back hurt terribly from the work he'd done in the quake. I'm getting awfully old for this, he decided. He wished he knew how to retire. He chuckled to himself.

****

At the edge of a deep canyon Kelsey turned slowly. He scanned the world for signs of civilization. Failing that, he walked along the ravine looking for a way down into the gorge.

Passing a rock he found Mordak, lying on his side, his hands clutching his stomach grotesquely. His face was turning bluer by the second. Kelsey remembered the poison. He remembered the horn phial. He pulled the small container from under his shirt and, forcing Mordak's mouth open, poured all of the powder onto his tongue.

Mordak shook his head once, violently, trying to clear it. He shivered, trying to push himself back, away from Kelsey. Already he was looking better.

I should've let it run its course, Kelsey realized. Maybe I could've saved Salia from her fate. But it was already done. Mordak was recovering. Kelsey shook his head slowly. That's how it is with fate, I guess.

****

<u>XV</u>

Both Kelsey and Mordak held sling shots. Not the elasticized ones of Kelsey's childhood, but the old kind; long cords with a little saddle to hold a stone.

Sound carried well in the still air and the dry, cracked earth crunched as they circled.

Mordak looked young and healthy to him, dangerously so. He wondered how he looked to his adversary. "Mordak?" he called out. "Are you calm, now?"

"Who the hell are you? Why do you keep calling me by name?"

"I'm Kelsey Darson," he shouted. "We are much the same, you and I."

"I think not." Mordak said.

"You'd be surprised. Or you will be."

There was a silence then as they looked at each other, neither of them swinging for an attack.

"Look, Mordak, this probably won't mean anything to you right now, but I have to say it anyway. It may make you a little less miserable down the road somewhere. Try to remember it."

"Why should I trust you? Why should I even listen?"

"Because I have nothing against you. I have no reason to lie to you. I've forgiven you. Long ago, it seems now."

"You've forgiven me? You're a madman, Darson."

"Not any more, Mordak. And you will be a madman, too, some day."

Mordak shook his head in disbelief . . . in distant disbelief.

****

The service was good and a blaze heated the room from a central fire place.

Kelsey sipped something that was quite like scotch and felt the burn as it slid down his throat.

He noticed, through the glass he held, that his palm was dry and calloused. He set down the drink and looked at his hands. They were longer than he'd remembered them. His knuckles knotted and his tendons cast shadows even when his fingers were not flexed. He flexed and the shadows deepened.

The reflection in his butter knife showed his hair was almost entirely gray. His face was gaunt and his eyes deep set.

Salia joined him at the table and he beamed at her. "You look so young," he said.

She bit her lip and stared. He was a little worried. Did he look so awful to her? He had to say something, so . . . "I think it's almost over for me, you know?"

She flinched as though there had been a loud sound. She spoke softly. "I think so," she said. "I've only seen you like this once, and -- and --"

"I died?"

She nodded and tears welled. She looked out at the pedestrians beyond the glass.

"It's okay, Salia. Whatever happened it's okay. I love you. I always have. And now I get my chance to say goodbye before I go."

She nodded. "I love you, too, Kelsey. I love you madly. I didn't get a chance to tell you before -- before --"

"I died?"

Again she nodded.

"You're telling me now. It's okay. You're telling me now."

He reached out and pulled her to him. He held her tightly. People looked at the unusual couple, he so old, she so young. Some of them passed judgment without enough information.

Something nagged at Kelsey. Something important. He remembered reminding himself to tell her something. What was it?

"What's the matter, Kelsey? You're distracted."

"There's something I'm supposed to tell you. I can't remember."

She began to seem removed to him, as though an invisible wall had sprung up between them or a sand-storm obscured his view. He remembered.

"When you see the sand dragon," he told her, "get down. Keep low."

"What?" She asked. "Why?"

"It breathes--"

****

Kelsey expected that he was falling now to the place with the field of poppies. The image had stuck in his head when he had heard it and only later had his subconscious sorted out its significance.

But there were no poppies. There was no field. Just an odd clearing in the midst of a damp jungle. His bones ached despite his gentle landing. He ran a thinning hand through thinning hair. He hoped he would find no crisis here.

"Kelsey. I never expected this."

He turned, and he was as surprised as his old nemesis. The two old men looked at each other. There was no reason to fight, no need to fear each other. Each had killed the other off long ago. There was both sadness and joy in the eyes of each man.

Kelsey reached out a hand and Mordak took it. They did not shake, they just stood that way, gripping each other's hands for a long, long time.

"I'm sorry I killed her, Mordak."

"And I'm sorry for-- for what I did. For everything."

"I know. We were fools. Both of us."

"We were young." He said. "We were so young."

"I'm fading. You seem far away."

"Do I?"

"I think I have to go meet you in a field of poppies."

Mordak nodded. "I expect so. I'll see you by the Oak tree."

"I guess you will."

****

There was no breeze. Kelsey had never seen the pond so still. For all her age, Salia had never been so beautiful to Kelsey. From her eyes he could tell that her thoughts were much the same. They held hands and gazed into each other's tired, happy eyes.

"I didn't know we'd get to see this place again."

"Neither did I."

They kissed. They kissed well. They had been kissing like this, it seemed, all their lives.

He led her to their favorite soft place on the slope. He was a little ashamed of the dry, roughness of his hands, of his bony fingers and thinning hair, but because he found her so beautiful he got past it and caressed her more sweetly than the breeze.

They made love for hours, kissing and touching and loving for old times, and for the moment, and for eternity.

****

Kelsey was sure he had fallen, and yet the pond was still there. The breeze had picked up a little, and the air grown a little more chill, but the pond was still there.

"Hey, Kelse!" Salia greeted him brightly. "You're looking good." Right down to the finish he was discovering firsts. He had fallen to the same place twice in a row. That had never happened before.

"I'm looking old," he said.

"Well, yes. But good. You look good old."

She was so young, so alive. There was no bitterness in her eyes yet and he knew what had not yet happened. He knew that when it did happen he would be outside the door, unable to protect her. He looked away and tears began to stream down his face.

She sat with him then and put her arms around him. There, by the pond, he bawled like a baby and could not tell her why he cried.

****

<u>XVI</u>

Though he felt somewhat weak and very tired, Kelsey did what he could to help the war effort, firing his heavy weapon into the oncoming mob, piecing out what he could of the political situation from his surroundings.

He realized, for the first time ever, that he had no way of knowing the attackers were not the good guys.

I'll bet, he thought, they think they've got a damn good reason for this invasion. Seeing the eyes of a young man in the attacking crowd, Kelsey lowered his weapon and let it fall to the ground before he fell away.

****

Kelsey's sword arm was not as quick to respond as it had once been, but as there was no field of poppies he knew he could not let Mordak kill him. Not here. Not just yet.

****

There they were. Just down the slope from him. Kelsey walked toward the poppies happily. The Game would come to an end. It had finally come to make sense. All the little pieces of the puzzle had fallen into place. Every effect had its cause. Every reaction had, eventually, come to have an action. He smiled as he walked and wondered if the euphoria was created by his final understanding of the Game, his knowledge that he had, at last, come to the end of it, or if it was simply a result of airborne opiates. He wondered. He did not care.

Mordak would be here soon and he would depart this world . . . all these worlds. He was glad he had not allowed himself to be killed in that last place. This was a good place to die.

Salia walked with him, then. She was not very old. "You're old, Kelsey."

"I know," he said.

He thought about what he would write in his journal if Mordak took a while to show up. Something dawned on him and he stopped walking. He began to laugh.

"What's funny, Kelse?"

"I thought I had the whole thing figured out. Just now. I thought it had finally come together."

"And?"

"There's no pattern. There's no explanation for it all. And it's about to be my own fault."

"How do you figure?"

"Here," he said and handed her his journal. "I lost this a while back. Return it to me when you can."

"Okay. No sweat."

He laughed again at the little paradox he had just created. Better to leave one loose end than never to get his journal back when he had lost it. He remembered his joy at its return and thanked himself for giving himself that gift now that he had received so long ago.

"Wait here," he told Salia. "I think I have to do this on my own." But in truth he did not want her to be too close. He did not want her to see this too clearly.

Amongst the poppies he sat down. He knew now why Mordak had leaned against that tree waiting for him that way. When he died he did not want to fall.

Salia watched from the place where Kelsey had told her to. Mordak grew quickly into place as if falling forward from some great distance. Even from so far away she could see the rage in his eyes. She feared for Kelsey's safety and began to run toward him even as she saw Mordak deliver a crushing truncheon blow. Kelsey slumped over, his bright blood clashed against the summer colored poppies.

"You bastard," she screamed. "You son of a --"

Mordak turned toward her, but already the world was receding too fast and him with it.

****